THE NINE FLORA McFLIMSEY BOOKS
Miss Flora McFlimsey and the Baby New Year
Miss Flora McFlimsey's Birthday
Miss Flora McFlimsey's Christmas Eve
Miss Flora McFlimsey's Easter Bonnet
Miss Flora McFlimsey's Halloween
Miss Flora McFlimsey and Little Laughing Water
Miss Flora McFlimsey and the Little Red Schoolhouse
Miss Flora McFlimsey's May Day
Miss Flora McFlimsey's Valentine

Miss Flora McFlimsey's Halloween

By
Mariana

Lothrop, Lee & Shepard Books   New York

ILLUSTRATIONS BY MARIANA RECREATED BY CAROLINE WALTON HOWE.

Copyright © 1972 by Mariana, 1987 by Erik Bjork.

First Edition   1 2 3 4 5 6 7 8 9 10

Library of Congress Cataloging in Publication Data
Mariana. Miss Flora McFlimsey's Halloween.
Summary: A doll's Halloween adventures are interrupted by the news that her house is invaded by goblins. [1. Halloween—Fiction. 2. Dolls—Fiction.] I. Title. PZ7.M33825Mk   1987   [E]   86-15270
ISBN 0-688-04549-9   ISBN 0-688-04550-2 (lib. bdg.)

Pookoo Cat was brushing his whiskers in front of the mirror in the dollhouse. He was singing softly to himself:

"Ho for the Milky Way and saucers
    of milk in the sky
For good kind cats like I."

"You should say 'like me,' not 'like I,'" said Miss Flora McFlimsey.

"I like it better my way," replied Pookoo as he straightened his collar.

"Are you going out this evening, Pookoo?" she asked.

"Yes," answered Pookoo. "I have an appointment with a witch."

Miss Flora McFlimsey gave a little gasp. She had once seen a picture of a witch riding on a broomstick, and she'd thought, I wouldn't like to meet *her* after dark.

"It might not be safe, Pookoo," she said, "to go out to meet a witch at night. It would be better to stay right here in the dollhouse."

"Nonsense!" said Pookoo. "This witch is a friend of mine. This is Halloween and no time to stay at home. It's a night for adventures, a night when anything can happen."

Miss Flora McFlimsey sat very still, thinking. It might be dangerous, but she hadn't had an adventure in a long time, and...

"Pookoo," she said, "may I go too?"

"Certainly not!" replied Pookoo. "This is no night for dolls to be out. Besides, you might wiggle."

"Wiggle!" exclaimed Miss Flora McFlimsey.

"Yes, wiggle and fall off."

"Fall off what?"

"The witch's broomstick. That's what we're going to ride on."

Just then there was a scratching on the roof and a shrill whistle down the chimney.

"There she is now," said Pookoo.

"Please let me go too," cried Miss Flora McFlimsey. "I won't wiggle."

"Well, if you promise not to wiggle, and to behave as well as I do, I'll ask her if you can come along," replied Pookoo. "Now hurry!"

Miss Flora McFlimsey hastily put on her hat with the plumes and her blue velvet cloak and her white kid gloves. She opened the door and she and Pookoo slipped quickly out into the night.

With one jump Pookoo was on the roof of the dollhouse. He reached down a paw and helped Miss Flora McFlimsey to climb up.

The moon was shining brightly, and by its light Miss Flora McFlimsey could make out the figure of a little old woman wearing a tall hat and a long black cape.

She was bending over a broomstick, muttering something that sounded like:

"Mumblety, jumblety, tippledetay,
Rumplety, rumplety, ripplederay."

"This is Miss Flora McFlimsey," announced Pookoo. "She'd like to come along."

The witch peered down at Miss Flora McFlimsey with her little beady eyes and muttered, "She's welcome to come along, if I can get this stick to fly—it's that contrary, and on Halloween of all nights!"

"I'll just give it a scratch or two," said Pookoo. "There's nothing like a good scratch to start things moving."

"Shh–sh–h," said the witch. "Better to coax it." She began to whisper:

"Beautiful stick, my pet, my pride,
  Fly, fly, fly high in the sky."

The broomstick shook a little. Then it rose straight up in the air.

The old witch was astride it in two winks. Pookoo leaped on in front of her—and Miss Flora McFlimsey scrambled on behind.

Up they went, high over the roof of the dollhouse and over the tops of the trees.

Pookoo was waving his tail and singing:

"Ho for the starry sky
  And witches and cats what fly."

Miss Flora McFlimsey tried to say, "It's *who* fly, not what fly." But her little voice was lost in the night wind and the shrill whistling of the witch.

She held on tight to the old witch's cape and tried not to wiggle.

Curious things were moving about in the air and on the ground.

They passed over Oliver Owl's hollow tree and Peterkins's little burrow.

Higher and higher went the broomstick. Miss Flora McFlimsey shut her eyes tight. Pookoo was right. It was no night for a doll to be flying about in the sky. What if we should bump into a star, she thought.

Something was crawling up her back. Now it was on her shoulder. She could feel its claws through her velvet cloak.

A little squeaky voice spoke in her ear. "Don't be afraid, Miss Flora McFlimsey. I'm here."

"Oh, Timothy Mouse," cried Miss Flora McFlimsey. "Is it you?"

"Yes," answered the squeaky voice. "Luckily for you, I was on the roof of the dollhouse, looking at the moon, when I saw you getting on this broomstick. I quickly hid in the broomstraw so that I could go with you and protect you. Be bold, I always say. Just look at me, a mouse on a broomstick in the sky, in the company of a witch, and— what is worse," he whispered, "—a cat! But am I afraid? Not I, not T. Mouse!"

Just then something flew close beside them in the darkness. It went "Who-o-o-o-o-o-o-o."

Timothy Mouse at once disappeared into a fold in Miss Flora McFlimsey's cloak.

Miss Flora McFlimsey gave
a little scream and let go her hold
on the witch's cape, and at that
same moment she — *wiggled!*
And off she tumbled!

Down,

down,

down,

blump!

Right onto a grassy spot on the ground!

The moon went behind a cloud. Miss Flora McFlimsey lay still for a minute. Then the moon peeped out again, and she sat up and looked around.

There she was, goodness only knew where, and all, all alone!

But, no! She heard a faint, muffled squeak. A little face and two big ears peeped out of the pocket in her cloak.

"Don't be afraid, Miss Flora McFlimsey," said a shaky voice. "I'm here."

"Timothy Mouse!" Miss Flora McFlimsey cried. She tried to take him out and hold him in her hand. But something was fluttering just over her head and making a queer sound—"Hoot, hoot, hoot, hoot!"

Timothy Mouse disappeared back into the pocket of Flora McFlimsey's cloak.

There were more flutters, and a small owl lit beside her.

It was little Oscar Owlet, who lived with his uncle, Oliver Owl, in the big hollow tree.

He was so excited he could hardly speak. But he managed to stammer, "Oh, Miss McFlimsey, Miss McFlimsey, something terrible is happening! My uncle Oliver had to be away tonight on important business. So he left me at home to watch out for spooks and goblins. I was sitting just inside our hollow tree, listening, when five little green goblins came and sat on a low branch. And, oh, Miss McFlimsey, what do you suppose I heard those goblins say?"

He came closer and whispered, "They were planning to break into the dollhouse and steal things and carry you off with them!

"When they started for the dollhouse, I waited a little while so that they wouldn't know I was following them. Then I flew after them. I peeped in the window and, oh,

Miss McFlimsey," he stammered, "those wicked goblins were sitting in your rocking chair and looking at themselves in the mirror and drinking Pookoo's milk, and worst of all, they had opened your trunk and were trying on your clothes."

He began to fly helplessly around in a circle, crying, "Hoot, hoot, hoot!" Then he lit on a branch and tucked his head in among his feathers.

There was a tiny squeak, and Timothy Mouse's little head appeared. "I heard what that stupid owl said," he whispered. "I never cared much for owls. But listen carefully. I have a plan. Just leave everything to me.

"I have, as you know, a little private entrance into the dollhouse. I will run quickly through the grass and over the fields and enter by my secret door and find out just what is happening. I'll order those goblins to leave at once. I'll say 'Scat!' to them.

"Don't be afraid, Miss McFlimsey. Just trust T. Mouse."

Miss Flora McFlimsey tried to catch him, but he slipped away and was gone.

"Oh, dear," cried Miss Flora McFlimsey. "Suppose those goblins carry Timothy Mouse off with them! If only I knew where Pookoo went. He would know just what to do." She began to cry.

There was a whir-r-r of wings and a large owl lit beside her.

"It's Uncle Oliver!" cried little Oscar Owlet, fluttering down.

"I'm on my way to the Witches' Ball," explained Oliver Owl. "I just stopped off to see if all was well."

The Witches' Ball! Then Miss Flora McFlimsey remembered.

That was what Pookoo had called out when they were riding on the broomstick. "On to the Witches' Ball!"

Pookoo must be at the ball that very moment!

"If only I could get there," she thought, "and tell him to come quickly to the dollhouse before it's too late."

"Mr. Oliver Owl," she said, "will you let me ride on your back to the Witches' Ball?"

"I must fly very fast," said Oliver Owl. "The time is short. The midnight hour, when all witches must leave the earth, will soon be here. Can you sit still and hold on tight and not..."

"Wiggle?" added Miss Flora McFlimsey quickly. "Yes, I promise!"

Miss Flora McFlimsey climbed onto Oliver Owl's back, and in a few moments they were flying swiftly along, with Oscar Owlet close behind.

Soon they could see a fire burning and hear fiddles playing and see dancers moving about in the firelight.

Oliver Owl lit in the shadows. Miss Flora McFlimsey slid off his back and ran in among the dancers, looking for Pookoo.

Strange creatures were
dancing to the music. A little
spook wearing a white
sheet, with tall furry ears,
said, "Good evening,
Miss McFlimsey."

"Peterkins!" cried Miss
Flora McFlimsey.

"How did you ever
recognize me?" asked Peterkins.

There was Tuffy Puffin
dancing with Peterkins's
aunt, Mrs. Cottontail, and
Danny Beaver dancing
with a green goblin, and
Fernando Fox with Mrs.
Porcupine, and the three little
porcupines. But where was
Pookoo?

Miss Flora McFlimsey saw the old witch stirring something in a big pot over the fire. A black shadow sprang up at her side. It was Pookoo!

Miss Flora McFlimsey ran toward him. "Oh, Pookoo," she cried, "come quickly, hurry, hurry! Goblins are in the dollhouse!"

She explained how she had fallen off the broomstick, and how Oscar Owlet had found her and had brought her word about the goblins, and how Timothy Mouse had gone alone to order them out.

"It all comes of wiggling," said Pookoo. "If you hadn't wiggled and fallen off the broomstick, you wouldn't have been talking to that silly owl and that crazy little mouse!"

"But Oscar Owlet says they have opened my trunk," exclaimed Miss Flora McFlimsey, "and are trying on my clothes!"

"You shouldn't be so vain, Miss McFlimsey," replied Pookoo, "always thinking about clothes!"

"And I'm sure they're holding Timothy Mouse prisoner."

"That's a very good idea," said Pookoo. "If they'll just keep him there until..."

"And they're drinking your milk."

"What!" cried Pookoo. "Drinking my milk! Well, of all things! We must leave at once," he said to the old witch. "Quick, there's no time to lose. To the dollhouse!"

The witch mumbled:

"Mumblety, jumblety, tippledetay,
  Rumplety, rumplety, ripplederay,"

and jumped on the broomstick.

Pookoo sprang on behind her, and Miss Flora McFlimsey managed to take hold just as the broomstick rose clear of the ground.

"On to the dollhouse!" cried Pookoo, waving his tail.

The broomstick flew straight on over the trees and came down slowly right in front of the dollhouse.

"Advance with caution," cried Pookoo, leading the way.

They crept up stealthily and peeped in the windows.

The goblins were making merry, singing and dancing and standing on the table. One was wearing Miss Flora McFlimsey's Easter bonnet. Another was opening her pink parasol and another was smelling her little bottle of Eau de Cologne.

But far off a clock was striking: one, two, three, four, five, six, seven, eight, nine, ten, eleven, twelve. Midnight!

Out of the dollhouse came the goblins, tumbling through the windows and out the door.

The old witch gave a shriek and seized the broomstick.

Soon the air was full of elves and goblins and ghosts and witches, all flying from the earth.

"Goodbye, goodbye, my dears," cried the witch, "until next All Hallows' Eve."

They caught one last glimpse of her on the broomstick, clearly outlined against the bright moon. Then she was lost in the night.

Miss Flora McFlimsey and Pookoo stood looking up at the sky.

Just then a tiny object darted out of the dollhouse. It was Timothy Mouse.

"I said 'Scat!' to those goblins at twelve o'clock," he squeaked, "and off they went. Be bold, I always say. . . ."

Miss Flora McFlimsey hastily picked him up and hid him in the pocket of her cloak.

From the pocket she could hear him whispering squeakily, "Just trust T. Mouse."